Rejected Not Dejected
A Collection of Spurned Short Stories

Ryan G. Figueroa

To my dearest wife, Aleena.
You've never let me give up on myself. Thank you
for joining me on this crazy ride.

CONTENTS

CONTENTS

INTRODUCTION

"Our deepest fear is not that we are inadequate, but that we are powerful beyond measure."
- Marianne Wiliamson

"It seems to me most strange that men should fear; Seeing that death, a necessary end, will come when it will come."
- William Shakespeare

There is so much I want to say in this introduction that could probably take up quite a bit of space and time. I also acknowledge that many readers will skip right over this to immerse themselves in what they hopefully deem as at least decent storytelling. "Just get to the story, already!" I get it. I don't often read these myself, but when you put your heart and soul into something there's a compulsion to have to explain yourself. That being said, I'll attempt to keep this brief.

What follows is a compilation of original short, flash, and micro-fiction stories. I've included the original prompts for the stories for context. While they vary in length, genre, and style, the one thing they share is they are all rejects. They have all endured heartbreaking rejections by contests, magazines, e-mags, and podcasts. I know, "Why put a bunch of terrible stories in this book? Is this some desperate grasp for attention and significance?" And to that I say, Yes... in part. There's lots of underlying and deep-seated emotional points that would take tons of hours in a therapist's office to unpack, but for brevity let's just say this: I'm tired of playing it safe and doing what's comfortable, and if all this does is help one other person realize that they can too, then it will have all been worth it.

The first story I ever started, completed, and revised (multiple times) is the first story featured in this anthology. "The Earliest Hour" came from a prompt to "start your story with a sentence that is genuinely happy and uplifting with no hidden meaning. Then, end your story with the same sentence, only it is darker." It was also the first story I let anyone ever read. My brother and my wife were my first beta readers, and I was nervous. Turns out, they loved it. I then took another step and joined a writer's group. With some questions and some editing help, it got refined a little more.

In May 2020, right as people were realizing how big this COVID-19 thing actually was, I submitted "The Earliest Hour" to a short story contest. The winner was supposed to be flown out to London for some award, but I never heard back. I'm sure the Corona virus had at least something to do with that. It was after submitting this piece where I felt a sense of accomplishment. "The Earliest Hour" had been through so much revision and editing with my writer's group, I felt that I had to take the next step in putting it out there.

It was probably within a month that the ad came over Instagram. It was for a micro-fiction contest to tell a story in 100 words or less in 24 hours using the random genre, action, and word they would assign. I paid the registration fee and wrote my first microfiction piece, "Direct Consequences." It was my first official rejection, but I was invigorated. Writing towards a deadline was thrilling. I couldn't overthink my story and had to figure out how to be incredibly concise (for context, this paragraph is ninety five words).

I remember telling my wife first, and then one of my mentors that I was going to set a goal to enter five different writing contests by the end of 2020. Having already submitted two stories for two contests, I thought it was a reasonable stretch goal. And, through the same company that put out the 100 word microfiction challenge, I entered their flash fiction (1000 words or less), short screenplay (five pages or less), short story (2500 words or less), and micro-fiction part 2 (250 words or less)contests. "The Awakening," "Six Murders on the Brazos," "Frenzy," and "Destiny Has It" all came from the flash fiction part of the writing contests.

"Power Suit" and "Field Trip" are results from the short screenplay contest. The formatting is intentionally different from the rest of the stories as they are meant to be more like a script. You have permission now to skip past those if they are too difficult to read or get into.

"Destiny has It" was the second micro-fiction story contest that I actually missed the deadline for, but since I had written it, I wanted to include it. It's also a prequel to "Six Murders on the Brazos."

The most recent contest I entered was for the First Line Publication where the only real hard parameter was to start the story with the same first line, "Lily unlocked the back door of the thrift store using a key that didn't belong to her." I found it intriguing and decided to give my attention to it. It also got rejected. There are actually two versions to this story, the one that was submitted to the publication which is featured here, and a much longer (and currently incomplete) version. Perhaps I'll revisit that story as well someday. I wanted to do so much more with it then what my time and word count constraints allowed for. Sometimes, good is better than perfect and done is better than great.

Then there's Iggrash my dumb and wonderful goblin. "Iggrash the (Almost) Invincible " came to me by using a similar prompt format as the writing contests provided. Using free generators on the interwebs, I gave myself a random object, genre, and setting .

Both Iggrash the character and the story he occupies are rejects. This story is the only one featured that wasn't originally written for a contest, though make no mistake, it has received its fair share of rejections from various publications. It is also the only story where two different beta readers unbeknownst to each other stated they wanted to create fan art for the mishap goblin. Despite his goblin ways, I found myself really connecting with his silly ambitions and want to be seen for who he is.

I have thoroughly enjoyed the writing process of bringing these stories to life. They have all been through various revisions and publication submissions. Some of the editors and contest judges actually took the time to provide additional feedback which, to the best of my ability, has been applied and reapplied to many of these. If you are reading this, thank you. I hope that you find some enjoyment through these. And now, on with the show!

PROLOGUE
A CREATIVE'S LAST STRAW

To: ryansemail@email.com
From: everymag@email.com
RE: Your Submission

We appreciate the opportunity to read your work, but we will not be publishing your story. There was a lot we enjoyed about your piece, but unfortunately, it isn't right for us. Best of luck in finding a home for this piece.
Sincerely,
Editors and Staff of EveryMagazine

The sigh released his disappointment as Ryan dutifully moved the latest rejection email to his "Rejection Celebration" folder. The folder proliferated in volume from all the magazines, e-zines, and podcasts he had submitted his different stories to. The idea for the folder came from Stephen King who had, in his unknown days as a writer, hammered a spike into the wall with all the pink rejection slips he'd received. Ryan even took the time to print his rejection emails and mount them to his own cork board to visualize better the work and the discipline he put into his craft daily. Still, sometimes the disappointment crept in and sat on him like a stealthy sumo wrestler.

"Is this really even worth it? Shouldn't I just get a stable job with decent pay and good benefits that lets me provide for my family." That was his sensible voice talking; The sensible, safe, slightly cynical

voice that he just decided to name Chaz.

"Ok, Chaz," Ryan countered, "But, then what? If I live a life in the box and never do anything significant, what will have been the point? What will I have taught my girls?"

"But what if you fail?" Chaz asked. "Then I'll be exactly where I am now," Ryan continued, "At least I'll know that I've tried." "But it's just a waste of time, right? All these rejections are saying the same thing: 'The work isn't good enough.'"

Ryan pressed his fingers into his temples. The constant disappointment oftentimes made him question what he was doing. Tears welled up in his eyes taking in everything Chaz had said. It made sense; after all Chaz was safe and sensible. But, throughout his life, Chaz had often been the quiet guide.

All of this was new; This was the first time where Ryan had decided to truly step out. Another, quieter, voice spoke up. It was a voice that had been with Ryan well before Chaz ever came along. In fact, it had been with him before he was born. It was the very same voice that had spoken life into the very cosmos. With three simple words, a warm electric tingle spreads peace and power through Ryan's entire body, "You are worthy."

The pulsing energy of the Divine flowing through him, Ryan spoke aloud in his own voice, "Then I'll do it myself."

THE EARLIEST HOUR

START THE STORY WITH A PHRASE THAT'S GENUINELY POSITIVE. END THE STORY WITH THE SAME PHRASE THAT HAS TURNED DARKER.

The mountain air filled with the smell of fresh snow. The sun was nowhere to be seen. The birds had not yet begun to sing, and she had it all to herself.

For Juliana, the four o'clock hour beckoned her with its peaceful and still serenity. Many thought her crazy for willingly being up at an hour where only God and the godless were awake. She used to agree until one serendipitous mistake converted her. By forgetting a simple and arguably obsolete practice, she fell in love with the beauty of the early hour.

Juliana still used an alarm clock. She'd often sleep through her alarms on her phone, but the alarm clock's loud abruptness proved incredibly reliable. Every morning, the alarm clock launched her from slumber at five o'clock sharp. On this fortuitous morning, she woke up and went through her routine on autopilot moving through her morning rituals in just under an hour and a half.

The coffee wafted to her nostrils as the mug warmed her hands. The silence laid like a blanket over her ears while her actual blanket swaddled her safe and secure. She could not know how quickly the morning would snatch her safety away from her.

By 5:05 AM her coffee percolated while she finished her morning stretches and guided breathing. 5:15 AM made sure she'd showered and was doing her hair and makeup. As a beautician, she gave no less than thirty minutes for this part of her routine; Only two brands ever touched her face, MAC for the shows and expos and PUR for everything else. Her hair always wore the trendiest styles.

Afterward, she'd spend an average of twenty-ish minutes convincing her dog to use the bathroom. Her last fifteen minutes involved getting dressed and leaving no later than 6:30 am. With her hand on the doorknob, she noticed the clock on her phone read 5:23 am. Moments passed blankly before she realized her mistake: she'd forgotten Daylight Savings Time.

"Well I'm not lying down and messing up my hair," she said, then considered for a moment. She took her insulated mug and a blanket out to her backyard balcony surrounded by the mountains. For an unexpected hour, she escaped into the morning.

From that moment on and for the rest of her life, Juliana could not be convinced to start her mornings otherwise. For a brief hour every morning, she had nothing to do but exist with nature. She was determined to do this until the day she died.

Her working hours saw her as a hair and makeup stylist for the greater Boulder area. She spent eight years in LA learning from the best and working with true masters on A-list actors, musicians, politicians, and athletes. She loved LA, and would have likely stayed there forever until he forced his way into her life. The stalking and eventual physical violence had been enough to convince her to move. Boulder offered a do-over complete with gorgeous scenery and a far less saturated market where she established her own salon.

Juliana could not see beyond the treeline that surrounded her backyard which, under normal circumstances lent to her meditative mornings offering more stillness. She did not see the hungry and blood-thirsty eyes that waited and watched her.

Juliana often worked with the local drag show community. Her clients offered unique challenges including the Annual Celebrity Look-Alike Contest and Talent Show. After she'd finished her art, Beyonce herself would be hard-pressed to win against a Beyonce look-alike.

Outside of her salon, Juliana labored four days a week developing her body in MMA style fighting with her trainer, Patrice. She'd never allow herself to be the victim again. In the evenings, Juliana fed her mind with online Spanish and Business courses from Front Range Community College.

Delilah will be waking up soon. Juliana rolled her eyes at the thought of her dog. The daily battle of convincing the beast to go outside in the cold snow to use the bathroom would begin and then shortly after the rest of her morning routine would kick in. She was in no hurry to begin all of that as she breathed in the contrasting smells of steamy coffee with the crisp fresh air.

The predators in the thicket were in no hurry either. They knew how to wait for their prey to come to them.

Delilah and Juliana found each other when Juliana came across a man illegally selling German Shepherd/Wolf mixed puppies out of a box outside of his van.

As Juliana bent down to look at the pups, the man grabbed her by the hair attempting to yank her towards the van. Unfortunately for her assailant, Juliana had already been taking Brazilian Jiu-Jitsu with Patrice. In lightning response, her fist hammered the pressure point beneath his bicep while her knee introduced itself to his groin. He fell to the ground holding himself like a child who'd just wet himself. *I think he actually wet himself.* Juliana stood poised, daring him to make his next move. Like all cowards, his next move included fumbling into his van and driving off, leaving the box of puppies alone with Juliana. She took the box to the nearest animal shelter but not before locking eyes with the young pup that would become her Delilah.

On the normal and as early as 4:40 am, her beautiful mess of a dog would begin to stir, needing to go out though it seldom was an easy process. Delilah hated going outside to use the bathroom in the cold and snow. Unfortunately, most mornings in Boulder this time of year were both cold and full of snow. Delilah's first strategy at the sound of her master's calling was to dart under the bed. She'd whimper and whine as Juliana fumbled to put the leash on. Continuing her civil disobedience, she'd drop her body weight as Juliana attempted to drag her from under the bed. This tactic continued until Juliana dragged her to the door. Delilah's last resort included sitting on her haunches with a woeful and pathetic stare at her human. She'd much rather pee on the bathroom rug like a civilized dog.

As regular as clockwork, Delilah the big diva stirred inside. Juliana sighed hopeless affection for her pup as she sat her coffee down.

To Juliana's surprise, *the big diva's* drama was a lot less high maintenance than normal. Juliana got the leash on the first try and coaxed the beast from under the bed in a fraction of the time it normally took. Delilah *even* walked towards the door - more or less. *She must really have to go.* Of course, Delilah still vocalized her complaints, but Juliana had the hope that perhaps her dog realized the way of things. All in all, the time from Delilah's bed to the door was cut in half. Juliana found idol thoughts drifting back to her sanctuary on the porch.

Most days, this was a 30-minute ordeal.

The duo moved past Juliana's setup on the deck and cautiously down the icy and unforgiving steps.

After being subjected to do her business outside, Delilah huffed to her bed and buried herself in her blanket until Juliana brought her breakfast. Juliana would bring her breakfast with the same sarcastic tone, "Apologies, Your Majesty, Queen of the Domain."

Delilah's usual whimpering halted into alertness once her paws hit the snow-covered earth. Her ears pulled her head straight up and her nose sniffed the air until her eyes fixated at a point on the fence line. The hair on her back stood straight up and she bared her teeth.

Juliana froze on the last two steps with her companion's sudden shift in demeanor. Her goosebumps synchronized with Delilah's raised fur. Something was out there. *Rabbit?* The speed of thought canceled out that hope with two other simultaneous revelations:

Why isn't Delilah chasing it?

Because it's not a bunny.

The third through sixth thoughts fired like a machine gun: *What if it's a bear? Don't bears try to avoid people? What if it feels threatened? Get inside you fool!*

The last thought was enough to compel her to move up the stairs. That was, until she saw the disembodied eyes hovering over the snow and glowing in the moonlight like a phantom. Fear seized her and her thoughts left her. The eyes definitely belonged to something big, though seemed too low for a bear. The eyes' ferocity pierced Juliana's soul.

Delilah's deep and threatening growls forced Juliana to look down at the beast beside her, mild shock registering her dog's intense fierceness.

Juliana looked back towards the fence to see that her fear had multiplied as a new pair of eyes joined the first. Then a third and fourth. The eyes coordinated closer to the house.

An eighth thought came into Juliana's head that seemed impossible and obvious. A chill spread down her spine that had little to do with the cold. The idea frightened her more than a bear.

Wolves.

After the reintroduction of gray wolves to Yellowstone National Park in 1995, rumored sightings of wolves coming down from Wyoming popped up throughout the Northern Colorado area. Since wolves were most active at night and since the sightings were rarely confirmed, they had become similar to the legends of Bigfoot. *Time to wake up now, J.* She wasn't dreaming.

The eyes' skulked closer enhancing their silhouettes in tight formation. She'd seen plenty of foxes and coyotes around these parts, but these creatures came up to her waist. Juliana backed up the stairs, jerking Delilah's leash. Delilah, however, seemed rooted to the spot. *Where did this dog come from?*

Like lightning, the demon pack launched forward.

Juliana loved the way her house creaked underfoot the way old houses like hers do. She appreciated the accompanying smells that old houses provided. After a meditative morning, her day-to-day rarely reached stressful levels. She could handle anything. "**Don't sweat the small stuff**," Patrice would say, "**and it's all small stuff.**"

Juliana's instincts turned her rightfully and immediately to flight mode up the stairs towards safety. Unfortunately for her, Delilah's instincts turned her rightfully and immediately to fight mode towards the pack. Two forces pulled in opposite directions as the leash that hung around Delilah's neck clung tight to Juliana's wrist, pulling her backward.

One of Juliana's favorite parts of her routine was getting the morning paper. It gave her an excuse to go out the front door around 6:00 am. Incidentally, this happened to be the time her attractive neighbor who lived a mile up the mountain would be finishing her run. She always wore tight bright workout leggings and a windbreaker that made Juliana sweat just a bit.

The loud POP either came from Juliana's shoulder dislocating from the pull of the leash or from her ankle as her body weight rolled over it. As Juliana came to, the stars in her eyes swirled with the stars in the sky.

What happened? She felt like she did when she had too many Jaeger bombs at the last drag show. The cold crept up her backside and snow soaked her robe. Synapses fired all at once vying for her attention, but it was her ears that drew her focus first.

Juliana pretended to read her paper as her eyes watched for her neighbor coming around the curve of the road. It seemed her heart always kept time to her neighbor's steps. Often, the two women exchanged pleasant looks and nods, but one time Juliana swore she saw a wink and a flirtatious smile. She hadn't quite "come out" yet, and therefore the dating and relationship scene was one of the few areas in her life where Juliana lacked confidence. "One day," she'd say.

From her supine position, she craned her head toward the racket. The primal sounds of growls and gnashing of teeth belonged to two of the wolves fighting each other. The others maintained the perimeter; watching, yipping, and growling their approval as if they were watching a boxing match.

The sounds, cold, and pain slushed her brain around. *Where was Delilah?* As the two bodies of mass flailed about, Juliana saw a leash fly into the air from around one of the wolves' necks. *It can't be.*

The two beasts broke apart and circled each other, giving Juliana time to process the scene. Delilah, her Delilah, was fighting a boulder of a beast and was somehow holding her own.

Why aren't the other wolves attacking? As her senses sharpened, her mind dragged out a memory from some nature documentary she'd seen before and shoved the word through her mouth in a surprised whisper, "Alpha."

Her prissy pup was fighting the Alpha. Juliana's love implored her to help while her instincts begged her inside, but her injuries and shock negated either from happening.

The two creatures flung themselves at each other again in a blur. The minutes passed through molasses in eternity while she watched Delilah make her stand. She watched with the morbid fascination of witnessing a fatal car wreck. She could not tell which was her dog.

The moonlight silhouetted tufts of fur flying into the air. Teeth snapped and ghastly howls boomed like thunder. Then, the death rattle silenced them all.

One of the creatures managed to grab the other by the throat and bit deep. The final screech emitted deep from the loser's soul. The vacant furry mass went limp in the victor's jaws. Juliana closed her eyes tight as the deathbed howl reverberated in her spine. *Delilah's dead.*

With her eyes closed, her other senses sharpened. The snow pushed at every nerve on her back. The silence pulsed in her ears and reverberated in her spine. Her arm and leg screamed in pain.

Silence? Juliana hadn't realized how much noise the two fighters and the surrounding wolves were making until they weren't anymore. *Oh shit.*

With Delilah dead, nothing stood between the predators and their prey. Their prey, who had been too wounded and too stupid to flee and now lay with her eyes closed like a scared child under the covers. Their prey who'd practically invited them to dine on her entrails. She sensed them surrounding her, drool dripping from their teeth. She wanted to keep her eyes closed, but morbid curiosity forced them open. They hovered, their primal hunger palpable.

The Alpha moved closer as the others stayed back. Fresh blood dripped down its nose from the fresh scratch over its eye. She closed her eyes, dreading to see what came next.

The passing moments seemed frozen with the snow and ice, yet the wolves still withheld themselves.

What are they waiting for? She opened her eyes. The Alpha's nose hovered close to her face and throat.

"WHAT ARE YOU WAITING FOR?" she screamed, hoping to either scare them away or provoke them to attack, though neither happened. The Alpha flinched slightly at the sudden outburst but otherwise maintained its proximity.

It just seemed content to stare at her, until it moved in suddenly. Juliana closed her eyes, refusing to watch or scream. *Oh God, this is it. Forgive me Father for my sins. Will my life flash before my eyes? When will anyone find my body? What is going on?*

This last thought forced her eyes open to find the other wolves had disappeared back into the cover of the wilderness. The Alpha maintained its gaze and Juliana finally looked it in the eye. She expected malice or hunger, but saw something different; It looked sad and somehow familiar.

Satisfied, the great wolf turned its head to make its way towards the treeline. The mangled leash around its neck brushed Juliana's face. *Leash?* Where her previous thoughts came quickly, this one seemed to stick to her synapse before registering the impossible.

"Delilah?" Her master's calling halted the beast mid-step and out of habit almost turned her head. Instead, she kept her head aimed at the spot where the wolves had come from. She couldn't turn back now.

Juliana followed her dog's line of sight and gasped, "Oh my God!" Three pairs of menacing eyes waited in a deja vu moment. Juliana realized what Delilah already knew, "It's a test." Delilah continued her deliberate walk into the darkness. One by one, the eyes blinked into nothingness following her.

Her brain muddled through the recent events. Her eyes wandered until they landed on the heaping mass of the former Alpha. The moonlight highlighted some of the gore.

Juliana moved her head back to find sad eyes reflecting the moonlight. "Goodbye," she whispered and Delilah turned for the last time.

Despite her current predicament, incredulousness shook Juliana's head, "Q-queen of her d-domain." The stuttering surprised her. With the most imminent threat gone, her body reminded her of the next one. Processing her predicament felt daunting: the cold seized her, her arm couldn't lift itself, and she laid on her back facing the wrong way from the stairs. There was, of course, the stairs themselves. She shivered with each syllable, "G-gotta g-get ins-s-side." She didn't know it, but she was in the throws of her own personal Thermopylae; her Alamo.

Panic sought to overwhelm her. *I'll never make it. I can't do this. How will I survive? I just want to...* Another inner voice broke through her panic with gruff determination, impatience, and full of love; **"You can whine or you can win, but you can't do both."** Though far from angelic, Patrice's voice would be Juliana's savior.

"The greater the obstacle, the more glory in overcoming it." Juliana nodded in affirmation. Her mentor had always been the grittiest, strongest, and most influential woman she had ever known. She was never in short supply of inspiring quotes either. This came from Moliere. "Okay, Patrice, let's do this," Juliana said.

First obstacle: turning over. Her dislocated shoulder promised to make this difficult. Attempting to rock her body with her useful limbs onto her chest was met with avid complaints as the sensation of a thousand needles prodding through her arm spread throughout her body. Gasping for breath, she focused on not passing out. Gritting her teeth she pushed again, quicker and more determined than before. This time she found success for lack of a word.

Pinning her arm under her body weight, the pain of needles turned into a sensation of a swarm of furious fire ants furiously eating her arm from the inside. **"You are tougher than life is painful!"**

There had to be a personal trainer/public speaker's handbook somewhere with all these sayings. Still, it kept her moving.

"FUCK!" Channeling her inner Amazon, Juliana lifted her body and swung her arm out from under her. The world darkened around her and the stars faded from sight.

"You rest when I tell you to!" Juliana snapped back to consciousness at Patrice's command. Her exposed and soaked backside quaked against the cold air and the numbness in the tips of her fingers and nose indicated the early stages of frostbite. *Not good.* Pulling herself up onto her knees left her right arm dangling under her like Delilah's tattered leash.

Juliana shuffled around towards the stairs; Those damned stairs. Like Brutus to Caesar, they seemed to invite her in only to bring her death. She reached out to grab the railing with her strong arm. Thirteen icy steps stood between her and safety.

Out of habit, Juliana pulled herself to her feet when her ankle complained painfully of its uselessness. Her right leg buckled, but she managed to reaffirm her grip on the rail before falling. She clung like a rock climber with a precarious finger hold.

Patrice spoke impatiently in her mind, **"You are tougher than life is painful. Now move!"**

"You try it sometime!!" Juliana spat back, forgetting that Patrice wasn't actually there. Juliana liked to think that if Patrice was actually there, she would have done more than just shout cliche words of encouragement.

The pain ebbed all over, but Juliana had known pain before.

Interestingly, this wasn't the first time she'd been close to death, either. The repressed thoughts of her L.A. stalker beating her to near-death because she refused to date him surfaced as a reminder; He'd clocked her with a right hook to the jaw and stabbed her through the ribs with a shard of glass. She knew the pain of ongoing reconstructive surgery and speech therapy. She knew the pain of having to heal both physically and mentally. Juliana was too tough then to die or give up. She'd be damned if she gave in now. To either Heaven or Hell, she shouted her declaration, "I. Don't. Quit!"

Leaning on the rail, she glared at the looming stairs before her with defiance. The stairs waited, almost smirking in return. *Hop up, maybe?* It seemed a decent idea in theory. Application proved treacherous. Hopping to the next step, her foot landed and slipped on the ice, bringing her body down hard on her knee with a heavy thud. Her grip held true, but her face grimaced at this new pain, "Well why the hell not?!"

She was not generally a crier, but hot tears forced their way out of her eyes and down her cheeks. She shouted to the heavens, "How 'bout a break?" Neither expecting nor receiving a response, she reoriented her focus. Her throbbing knee reinforced needing a better way up the stairs. With no other options, she opted for a modified crawl by pulling on the rail and raising her opposite leg, the one with the busted ankle. Raising her bruised knee to meet the first leg, the pain surged again. It didn't hurt like her shoulder or ankle, but it still did not appreciate having weight on it.

Her whole being protested her staggered climb, which felt less like stairs and more like climbing up a skyscraper. Dismay struck her when she realized that ten steps still loomed. *Only three steps?! I can't do this!* Her disembodied trainer disagreed, **"Push one more."**

Juliana lowered her head and closed her eyes. She found she could minimize the impact to her knee by using its corresponding ankle to leverage her weight off it while she pulled her other leg up. Finally, she found a slow rhythm: Left arm, pull. Right knee, push. Left ankle, push. **"One more."**

Left arm, pull. Right knee, push. Left ankle, push. **"Again."**

Left arm, shake. Right knee, wobble. Left knee - "Ahh!" The pain stopped her as her left knee took more weight than expected. More tears welled and her lungs felt like she was breathing fire. **"Again!"**

Left arm, pull. Right knee, push. "Doing okay," Juliana breathed. Right arm, smack. Her limp arm swung into the step in front of her, sending fresh shards of pain through her body.

Right ankle, "Shit!"

"There is no testament without a test. Focus, girl!" Patrice was right. She'd forgotten her rhythm through the pain and tried to balance with her busted ankle. She regained her composure for a moment. Then moved forward with her left knee, "NOPE!" She lifted the weight off her knee as the tears broke the dam of her eyelids. **"Five steps left."**

Juliana gasped for air, but the cold only reached in and squeezed her lungs. Despite the cold, sweat clung the hair to her forehead. She fought for consciousness as her whole body shook. She wanted to quit.

"If it doesn't challenge you, it won't change you." Her inner trainer's persistence forced Juliana to look around expecting to see Patrice in the flesh. She wanted to curse her for not doing more, but reality set her back to her task, "Fine," she gasped, "Left arm, pull."

"No matter how slow you go, you're still lapping everyone on the couch!" "Yah, yah." Right knee push.

The couch sounded wonderful. *I could just lie there all day with Delilah next to me...*

"NO!" Juliana exclaimed, snapping herself awake, "LEFT ANKLE, PUSH!"

"That's it! Again!" Left arm, pull. Right knee, push. Left ankle, push.

"The only easy day was yesterday!" Left arm, pull! Right knee, push!

"GAHH!" Left ankle, PUSH!

"Three... steps... left..." She lumbered up the next step with all the grace of a one-armed zombie who'd just had its legs chopped off. "Two…" Sweat poured, her body shook, and her breath shortened.

"The difference between 'try' and 'triumph' is a little 'umph!'"
Left arm, Pull! Right knee, Push! Left ankle, PUSH!

"That's it, girl. Don't stop when you're tired. Stop when you're done. JUST GIVE ME ONE MORE!"
Left arm, shake. Right knee, wobble. Left ankle, tremble.

All that was within, came out as she collapsed on the deck panting. The fatigue and cold had her, but relief flooded through her; she had made it. *Get inside. Call 911.* "Easy," she answered herself. Except that she needed to stand to reach the door handle.

Juliana re-affirmed her grip on the rail one more time. Her body convulsed like she was expelling demons. Her left arm and leg found renewed strength to pull her body past the pain in her knee. She only needed to reach out for the door. Somewhere, she thought of the fanfare from a Rocky movie.

After her routine, Juliana often got to town twenty minutes before opening the salon. Though she lived north of Nederland in a semi-secluded part of the mountains, it never took her more than 40 minutes to get into Boulder. Compared to living in L.A., this commute was a breeze.

She let go of the rail and reached for the door handle. Her right foot instinctively stepped down for balance; a mistake she'd made for the last time. Pain rocketed from her ankle as soon as her weight landed on it, and toppled her off-balance. Her trusty grip thrust out for counterbalance. *Oh God, No.* Her hand grabbed the rail, but her strength had left her. Unabated, her body continued its backward momentum.

Her commute only added to Juliana's serenity. The winding road passed through mountains with interesting local names like Mud Lake and Hurricane Hill. Driving east meant a beautiful sunrise often guided her into town like a beacon.

The world slowed down and her thoughts sped up.

She thought of Delilah: *I hope those wolves are nice to her.*

She thought of work: *Who will take my clients?*

She thought of family: *Mom and dad, I'm sorry I won't make it home for Thanksgiving this year. I'm sorry I didn't call more often.*

Juliana saw Patrice. Her dark skin contrasted against her amber eyes. Her sharp jawline smiled and her eyes were misty-eyed. She looked gorgeous. **"You gave it your best, girl. I'm proud of you."**

Juliana's shoulders hit the stairs hard and the momentum carried her legs over her head like a grotesque human Slinky. Her head followed her legs in pursuit down the stairs with a resounding SNAP. She found herself where she had started; on her back in the cold and unforgiving snow.

Juliana stared up at the now quickly fading stars. She couldn't move, but she didn't hurt; not anymore. A peace unlike any she had known before washed over her, encouraging her to close her eyes.

Through very few deviations, this was Juliana's routine since she discovered the beauty of 4 AM.

The mountain air filled with the smell of fresh snow. The sun was still nowhere to be seen. The birds had not yet begun to sing, and she had it all to herself.

DIRECT CONSEQUENCES

GENRE: DRAMA

WORD: GENTLE

ACTION: SPILLING A BEVERAGE

Jeremiah hoped this new foster family would be nicer. He rang the doorbell, and something inside shattered, causing him to flinch.

He'd misjudged the counter and saw the mug teeter downward.
The milk spewed.
The belt uncoiled from the belt loops; a snake ready to strike.
The glass tumbled beyond his grasp.
He gripped the refrigerator handle.
The glass and belt seemed to move as one towards their targets.
CRASH!
WHAP!
"Don't cry over spilled milk."

The gentle footsteps of his fate trod closer and a voice boomed, "That must be the new kid!"
The door opened to what God only knew and time would reveal.

THE AWAKENING

Genre: Political Satire

Object: Coloring Book

Setting: A Cemetery

For a moment, he stared at the crater in front of him. His eyes dragged from the hole to the stone planted behind it. The big capital letters "ARTHUR" preceded a smaller "JAMES" below it. Underneath, the date range "1961-2018" was emblazoned. "I'm dead," he observed almost nonchalantly.

A graveled shouting voice drew his attention. A rotting corpse proselytized through the cemetery, *"Prepare thyself, the Awakening is at hand! The living and the dead will be joined forever in eternity!"* A second zombie scuffled behind, with a more direct command, "Come on now, hurry up! Y'all rested long enough, and this blood moon ain't lastin' forever." They limped a few rows away repeating their calls. His lack of surprise surprised him, "Figures I'd be on this side of the zombie apocalypse."

Multitudes of putrid undead sprawled around him. Some, like him, stood fully out of their graves; looking as disoriented as he felt. A significant majority worked to pry themselves from the earth. One had most of her head and torso out, while another's feet were all that stuck through like two macabre stocks of corn.

Tremors shook his feet. A muffled, "HELP!" broke through the dirt two headstones away from him. He shuffled over to the site where a skeletal face and two skin-patched hands poked through the hard earth. "FLOYD, DOROTHY; 1849-1919" identified the newcomer. James pawed the dirt and grass around her face and soon her head and neck were free.

"What are you doing?" James turned toward the voice and saw a zombie leaning against a headstone thumbing through a coloring book. His skin and muscle tissue appeared mostly intact with only the beginning signs of deterioration and decay. His suit looked almost new.

"Call me Chip," the resting cadaver said, then repeated, "What are you doing?"

James indicated the obvious, "Helping."

"Why?"

"She asked for help... Where'd you get a coloring book?"

Chip shrugged, "My daughter colored some pictures for me and left this and some flowers." James turned back to Dorothy who had managed to free her shoulders with rags of a dress hanging off them. "Nobody helped me, by the way. Dug myself out on my own."

Before James could process what Chip was saying, the callers' voices echoed through the moans and groans, *"Prepare thyselves! The Awakening is at hand..."*

"I'm sorry no one helped you," James looked back at Chip. "Hell, I wasn't worried," He replied, "I was one of the first out too." *"...this blood moon ain't lastin' forever!"*

"Looks like this train's leaving the station," Chip commented.

James remembered his living self riding the Blue Line in Chicago. Just like the station, there was always so much hustling about, with some milling aimlessly while others booked it for the exit.

"It'd go faster if you'd help too," James responded. He realized that he may have had a filter in life, but there was little room for it here, it seemed.

"Why should I? It's not like I buried 'em or anything."

"Well, we should still help."

"Why?"

"Because they matter."

"Psh," Chip scoffed, "We all matter."

James and Dorothy had managed to free her past her exposed ribcage when they both stopped and looked at him.

A worm plummeted from Dorothy's jaw as it popped open to speak, "What does that even mean?"

"I'm saying, we're all here ain't we? Why should you get so much attention?" he responded.

"Maybe," her jaw grinded the words, "cause *I'm still in the dirt.*"

Not waiting for his reply she continued, "How can you say 'we all matter' but you won't do nothin' for anybody?"

"*I got myself* out. On my own. Without help," Chip stated, "As far as I figure, everyone else can pull themselves out too."

James and Dorothy exchanged glances. Dorothy shook her head and continued digging, the exposed section of her body already recomposing tissue and tendons over her bones as she shoveled the hardened earth around her. James doddled towards Chip and read the crisp epitaph, "TYLER, CHRISTOPHER 'CHIP'; 1987-2020."

James indicated towards Chip's headstone, "It looks like you and I died a lot more recently." "So?" Chip countered.

"So we started the afterlife with advantage, didn't we? It was easier for us."

"Hey now, I had dirt on me and a coffin to maneuver, same as everyone else!" Chip defended, "It's probably been at least a couple-uh years now, and it was heavy!"

"But," James continued, "compared to most everyone else here, that's no time at all."

James indicated towards Dorothy to emphasize his point and saw that she'd already freed what would have been her waist, "She's been dead for over a hundred years."

Chip repeated his argument, "So?"

James thought that if he rolled his eyes, they might fall out of his sockets. "*So*," he emphasized, "As heavy as ours was, it still hadn't settled as much. She's had all that pressing down and packing on her a lot longer. Think of all the roots, rocks, and grass to fight through."

Chip seemed more interested in the coloring book than anything James Arthur had to say but James persisted, "Plus, she didn't get to start with most of her muscle and tendons intact." He looked over Chip's nearly full form and added, "She's a lot stronger for it all. We'll be stronger with her."

Chip's shoulders squelched a shrug as he closed the coloring book. "Whatever guy, you're wasting your time." James watched briefly as Chip limped towards the exit before turning his attention back towards Dorothy, who had gotten out past her hips.

Like Chip, a good many of the uprooted listed past their still-planted fellows, while some had taken up a similar cause to help unearth them. "We gotta lot of work to do."

SIX MURDERS ON THE BRAZOS

GENRE: HORROR

OBJECT: A FOSSIL

SETTING: A BED AND BREAKFAST

"Where are we exactly?" "We *should* be almost there, let me check the map."

"I can't believe you convinced me to come out where we don't have phone service."

"I think it's perfect. It'll be an unplugged weekend where no one can bother us. Look, there's the sign for it!"

The weathered hand-painted sign pointed to the right with a red arrow followed by blue letters:

B&B ON THE BRAZOS!
"Come and sit a spell!"
Next Right on Devil's Bend Rd

Ty's face smushed with distaste as he turned the wheel onto the dirt road, "Lesanne, couldn't we have just stayed in Mineral Wells for our 'cleansing weekend?'"

Lessane ran her fingers over her canvas rollbag and smiled, "We'll get out that way, but this place looked so promising. YOLO, you know?"

Devil's Bend Road turned the highway's smooth asphalt into a gravel trail barely big enough for one car to pass at a time. The road wound like a giant white snake and opened to a clearing. They parked next to three cars in the grass.

The three-story asymmetrical victorian loomed at them from the top of a hill with its white shiplap armor and wrap around porch. "It looks so cute," Lesanne commented. "It looks haunted," Ty replied. He shook his head and added, "Why are you white people like this?"

Though well-maintained for a B&B, the house slanted slightly towards the left. The dark windows watched like black eyes as the two travelers approached. The pillars separating the awning from the porch looked like teeth ready to bite down. Two dead oaks planted on either side gave the illusion of two monstrous hands with wiry fingers ready to snatch anyone deep into its horrid mouth.

A similar sign to the one they saw off the highway stood out front with the same blue painted words, "B&B ON THE BRAZOS," but underneath, "SIT A SPELL!" beckoned in a friendly tone. Ty grabbed his duffle and locked the car, shaking his head. Lesanne hooked her arm through one of his, holding her own bag in the other hand, grinning and bouncing towards the house.

A sudden gust of wind blew as they approached. Despite the heat of the August sun, a chill spread throughout their bodies.

The door opened within a second of Ty knocking. Before their eyes could adjust, a gruff and booming voice shouted, "WHOSDER?" The voice was so close it caused Lesanne to yelp and Ty to shuffle backward. A stocky and bleach-pale elderly man stepped into the light. His beady black eyes glared at them. A snarl plastered on his face as he lifted a fat arm to shield his eyes from the evening sun. He wobbled like an overgrown toddler.

Lesanne spoke timidly, "We have reservations for the weekend? It's under Murray?" The glint of the black eyes hovered blankly over her for several seconds as his tongue licked the top of his lip, making her feel like a hamburger just brought to a homeless person. Finally, he moved aside and indicated their welcome.

They stood in the living room surrounded by ancient dark chocolate furniture. The burgundy walls gave the illusion that it was much later than it was.

Two other couples meandered around the room with drinks in their hand. A middle-aged white couple seemed to be intently studying the giant grandfather clock while two college-age boys sat on the couch, leaning into each other and whispering intimately.

Their hostess glided to them, "Welcome to our home!" Her long and bony body seemed to be held together by sheer force of will. Her pale skin seemed to glow despite the room's dark interior. A single spiral-shelled fossil earring dangled from her right ear lobe.

She extended her arm and cupped Ty's cheek, "Such a beautiful strong man you are." Ty had the sensation of someone dropping an ice cube down the back of his shirt that made him go rigid. Lesanne clutched her canvas bag, fingering the snaps on it.

"Oh, forgive me," Mary said as she lowered her hand, "I'm

making you uncomfortable." Her eyes stayed locked onto Ty as she spoke to her counterpart, "Fred, take our guests' bags up." Her eyes slid towards Lesanne almost apologetically, as Fred clambered to pick up the bags. The canvas bag clung tight to Lessanne's grip.

"I've been lookin' out for him since Mama died in '95. He hasn't been the same since. I guess neither of us have."

The rest of the evening proved less eventful. Mary spoke to the guests about the amenities, where to get tube rentals, and the house rules, "Breakfast at 8AM if'n you don't sleep in. No loud music or tv from nine to nine."

Fred showed Ty and Lesanne to their room a little after quiet hours and hovered until Ty thanked him, "That's it tonight, Fred. We'll let you know if we need anything." Fred grunted an affirmation and shuffled down the hall. Ty closed the door and turned to Lesanne, "Well this place is creepy." Lesanne shrugged, "It looked better online."

"Still," Ty considered, "I think you're right about this being a cleansing weekend."

Ty unsnapped and rolled out Lesanne's canvas bag onto the bed. "Which do you want to do first?" Lesanne asked as Ty looked at the hardware gleaming from the moon shining through.

"We'll make the woman watch as we do her husband. Then the gay couple," Ty responded as he slid out the large vice, "You cut the phones?"

Lesanne smiled as she coiled razor wire in her gloved hands, "And slashed all the tires. Who's gonna be the fighter?"

Ty considered this, "I think our hosts will give us a surprise." He strapped a drilling hammer to his waist as Lesanne grabbed two giant meathooks.

"YOLO, right?" Lessane repeated.

"Right." Ty agreed.

FRENZY

Genre: Horror

Object: An Underwater Camera

Setting: A Frozen Body of Water

The -7°C Ontario morning bit through Alfie's thick layers, but to him, it felt like Christmas morning. "Hey Alf, come here!" His uncle John beckoned to him with a piece of wood modified with various gadgets on it. "What's that?" Alfie asked.

"Take a look," John responded and handed it to Alfie. The 2x4 had a stretched oval hole cut through the middle. On one side, a neon land survey flag lay pinned under a metal clip. A spring connected through the board to a spool and fishing line on the other side. Twisting the spool sprang the flag to attention like a Mountie. He looked from the trap to the freshly bored hole in the ice with understanding, "The flag lets you know when you caught something!" "You think that's neat," John grinned, "Check these out!"

John revealed five small black objects that looked like penlights with lenses. Alfie's mom, Lissa, smiled as her son's face contorted into excited realization, "Those are cameras?! Are we gonna put them in the water so we can see the fish?!"

"You betcha," John beamed, " We'll tie 'em to the lines and stream to the monitors in my bob-house."

'JONO'S SHAVED ICE (YELLOW FLAVOR SPECIALTY)' had already sent Alfie into uncontrollable child-like laughter watching his uncle park the shanty on the frozen lake. Now, giddiness bounced through him as he practically dragged his mother and uncle to the tiny shack.

Inside, the adults enjoyed their coffee while Alfie, engrossed with the monitors, drank cocoa.

"Thanks for coming out, John," Lissa said, "I couldn't have done it by myself. Not so soon anyway."

"Hey don't sweat it sis. I'm glad to be here..." "WOW!" Alfie interrupted, "There's so many!"

Lissa and John peered over, surprise spread over their faces as numerous elongated and spotted barracuda-like fish swam erratically around the five cameras, "I've never seen pike that active," Lissa remarked.

"Me neither," John pointed to one of the screens, "There's one on trap two, and the others are attacking it." "Like sharks," Alfie observed. Lissa nodded, "In a frenzy."

Outside, they ran and slid towards their upright flag when a shout turned John's head toward their neighbor who fought to draw the line up from his own trap.

"Bill's got one too!" John remarked as he ran towards his own line to salvage his catch. A second flag sprang to life near him, "Woowee, Lis, looks like they're really biting!" Surprise overcame elation when all of his remaining flags shot up simultaneously; neon green warnings before his death. "Have ya ever seen..." his words cut off as he turned toward Lissa who stood midway between him and the shanty, staring with her hands over her mouth and her eyes fixed in terror. Following her line of sight, Jono's jaw dropped at the sight of blood spurting from where Bill clutched his hand. A 42" giant pike flopped angrily on the ice, a human finger poking in its mouth like a cigar.

John moved to help until his eyes were drawn down to his feet where the ice darkened around him. The ice shook as the shadow spread. Once it hit Bill's hole, dozens of fish erupted from it like a geyser. The hole broke wider, simultaneously launching more fish and swallowing the people into the abyss.

Another fish eruption ignited from John's bore behind him. The pillar of fish rose into the air and the rupturing ice tossed him flat. "Get off the... Ahh!" A large flying pike launched itself at John and bit into his nose. John tried to pry the incensed fish off his face, but the creature clamped harder. The precarious ice chunk toppled, condemning John to the icy abyss.

"John!" Lissa shouted, but the cacophony of ice splintering and fevered fish rushed her, forcing her to flee.

Alfie wanted to run, but terror froze him in place as if he'd become a living block of ice that could only watch as Bill and then his uncle fall into the tumult. Finally, his mother's frantic "Run, baby!" over the deafening rumble thawed his legs into fleeing. Ice shards splintered in all directions, slowing their escape.

Lissa scooped Alfie like a rugby player snatching a footie as the ice snapped around her. She sank into the water and lifted her boy over her head with raw maternal strength flowing through her. Her feet lashed out in its own determined survival when it scraped something solid. *Was that land?* Stretching out, she felt the shifting earth below the surface. Finding solid purchase, Lissa launched to shore as the maddened mob cascaded around, teeth and fins cutting their faces and ripping at their coats. The lake did not want to give up its prey.

Backing out of range from the flying horde, the lake broiled as if hell itself was escaping. The churning rumble muffled the other anglers' screams, but only barely. "What's happening, momma?" Alfie asked, his face buried in her coat.

Tears shook her response, "I… don't know, honey." For a time, they held each other thankful to be alive. Lissa's mind cleared a bit to assess their situation, "We have to get to the ranger's station and report what's happened." Alfie's eyes never turned from the hysteria as he nodded his head. "Come on baby,I think Uncle John's four wheeler is close," Lissa nudged.

The heavy snapping of twigs moving towards them halted them in fear. Parting through the brush, an adult black bear lumbered into view, pinning mother and son between it and the mania rumbling behind them. Blood oozed from countless bite and scratch marks and whole patches of fur had been ripped from the beast's body. Alfie's voice shaking had nothing to do with the cold, "D-did the fish get him too?" Lissa's own voice quavered back, "It… was coming *towards* the lake."

"Then," Alfie hesitated, "what got the bear?"

As if to answer, the sound of scurrying swelled from all around them drawing nearer until the first squirrel emerged with fresh bear's blood and fur matted to its face and paws.

POWER SUIT

Genre: Sci-fi/Fantasy

Object: A Menu

Setting: A Jury Room

FADE IN:

INT. A JURY ROOM - DAY

Six Jurors sit in a drab jury room around a brushed steel donut shaped table. There is no evidence on the table, only a holographic projection coming from the middle. They watch clips of a trial as they deliberate.

On the projection, Prosecutor JAX WILLIAMS (40s, male, white, Type-A) grills RONI SALOMON (30s, female, dark-skinned, academic) who sits on the witness stand.

> JAX
> Miss Salomon. How long have you
> been registered?

> RONI
> Just at six months

> JAX
> And how many people would you say
> you have directly saved in that
> time?

> RONI
> (Looks up, calculating)
> About fifteen. Maybe twenty.

Jax walks across the floor to the witness stand, getting close to Roni.

> JAX
> And how many people have you
> harmed?

Roni shifts uncomfortably in her seat.

> JUDGE
> Please answer the question, Miss
> Salomon.

RONI
I... I don't know.

The holographic projection pauses with Roni looking distraught and upset. JUROR #1 (40s, male, boisterous) drops the remote to the recording.

JUROR #1
The answer's four, to be exact.
Four people got hurt by her
irresponsible behavior. I really
don't see the point of doing this
again. She's obviously guilty,
right?

JUROR #4 (30s, male, compassionate)
We're treatin' her like some
common criminal! This is Madame
Auspice, we're talkin' about righ'?
That woman was able to defend
herself against those thugs with
that ice pick Madame Auspice gave
her!

JUROR #1
Yeah, but she took that ice pick
from that man causing him to fall
down the mountain.

JUROR #3 (30s, female, defensive)
I mean, let's be fair, is that
really her fault! How was she to
know?

JUROR #6 (40s, female, intelligent)
She shoulda known! She invented the
damned thing after all.

JUROR #2 (20s, female, tired)
So what, she should've let that
woman get mugged...
(pauses)
...or worse?

JUROR #5 (60s, male, reflective)
Can we skip ahead to the menu
again?

Juror #1 fast forwards a few frames, pushes play, and drops the remote in an over-exasperated gesture.

The projection resumes with the smart suit of Madame Auspice at attention on a Bellman's cart, It hangs onto a hangar with a hang tag on the collar marked Exhibit A. The charcoal gray jacket and pants appear to be no more than a regular dress suit.

JAX
Can you please tell the court and
jury what the parameters of your
powers are?

RONI
I'm a technopath.

JAX
So you know how my phone is feeling?

Laughter comes from the courtroom.

JUDGE
(banging gavel)
Order!
(looks to Jax and points with his hammer)
Keep it professional Mister Williams.

For a brief moment, the projection shows Roni's eyes in anger and embarrassment. She adjusts and takes a breath before speaking.

> RONI
> I can create anything from mechanical parts, a
> motor, or a computer and I can operate any machinery
> regardless of my prior experience with it.

> JAX
> And this suit is...

> RONI
> It's my greatest invention. It's meant to
> anticipate an imminent need.

The holographic Jax walks to the suit. He stares at it like he's dissecting a frog.

> RONI
> The left sleeve button turns it on.

Jax presses the corresponding button and a slight hum turns on. He steps momentarily back from the suit.

> JUROR #3
> This is my favorite part.

> JUROR #5
> (to Juror #3)
> Shush!

The prosecutor hesitantly sticks his hand inside the coat pocket and pulls out a fancy leather bound fold up menu. The cover says Le Magnifique in scripty gold lettering.

Jax stares at it with a look of awe and surprise. A collective gasp is heard over the recording from those present in the courtroom.

The jurors, including Juror #1 lean forward in anticipation. Jax Williams forces his focus back to his prosecution.

> JAX
> (Holds the menu up high
> for all to see)

Miss Salomon, can you please tell
the courtroom what I have pulled
from your suit pocket?

RONI
A menu.

JAX
A menu indeed.
Now why would I pull out a menu from your suit pocket

RONI
It anticipates an imminent need.
(defiant smirk)
Are you hungry, Mister Williams?

Laughter again echoes through the chamber. The Judge pounds
his gavel again, bringing the courtroom back to order.

JAX
(Collects himself, looks at the menu, smiles knowingly)
Miss Salomon, this menu comes from
a real restaurant. Do you know the
poor soul that has been denied his
menu at this very moment?

RONI
(Hesitantly)
I...don't.

JAX
You don't. Do you have any idea
what's happening right now at Le
Magnifique due to the sudden loss
of a menu?

Roni drops her eyes. Her hands fidget with each other as sweat
beads on her forehead. She shakes her head to indicate 'No.'

CUT TO:

INT. LIVING ROOM - CONTINUOUS

WALTER (male, 50s, bitter) sits upright in a wheelchair. He wears a neck brace and his bruised face is lit up by the television. His dog JACKAL sits on the floor next to him.

> TELEVISION (O.S.)
> Breaking News. Roni Salomon, aka
> Madame Auspice was found guilty on
> four counts of negligence and
> disregard to human life. In lieu
> of jail time, she was sentenced to
> twelve years in indentured
> servitude where her time will be
> spent working with The Hero
> Registration Authority developing
> further technological enhancements.
> Investigations continue in other
> super-heroics...

Walter clicks off the television in anger.

> WALTER
> Fuck that. She puts four of us in
> intensive care and Madame <u>Hospice</u>
> gets a slap on the wrist?

Jackal slides his head into Walter's lap and whimpers. Walter pets him automatically.

> WALTER (CONT'D)
> She took everything from me.

Walter looks at his wall. The various framed magazine covers illustrate a few of Walter's achievements in ice-climbing.

WALTER (CONT'D)
She literally took it from me.

His eyes continue along the wall to a newer section of newspaper clippings of Madame Auspice's heroics. A pocket knife sticks through the chest in one of the pictures.

Walter bares his cracked and missing teeth. The bruises highlight the menace in his eyes.

FADE OUT.

FIELD TRIP

Genre: Action/Adventure

Object: A Lunchbox

Setting: A Desert

FADE IN:

INT/EXT. A SCHOOL BUS - DAY

SOFIA ESPERANZA (female, 13, Hispanic, overweight, insecure) stares out the window of a school bus. West Texas plateaus roll along outside.

Inside, the chatter of thirty 8th graders echoes noisily. AMELIA RUIZ (female, 13, Hispanic, pretty, smart, mean) snickers with her twin brother EMIL (male, 13, Hispanic, handsome, vain) as they cast side glances at Sofia.

> AMELIA
> (TO EMIL)
> She's so pathetic, watch this.

> Amelia leans over the back of the seat
> and tosses a snack cake at Sofia.

> AMELIA
> (CONT'D)
> Hey Sofa. Why don't you shove that
> all in your mouth?

Sofia looks at the treat with unease.

> SOFIA
> I don't want to.

> AMELIA
> My brother wants to see you do it.
> He thinks it'd be pretty cool.

Sofia glances at Emil who flashes a smile. She smiles back, opens the snack cake and crams the entire pastry in her mouth.

A GIRL next to her points and shouts.

> GIRL #1
> Oh-Em-Gee! I can't believe she
> actually did that! Disgusting!

Other kids join in the laughter. Emil's face changes to horror while Amelia grins and stares. Sofia looks down at the floor, her hands fidget with the empty wrapper.

CUT TO:

INT/EXT. A SCHOOL BUS - CONTINUOUS

The students exit the front of the bus and exchange thanks and jokes with the bus driver JEFF WALKER (30s, white, fit, jovial). Sofia shuffles up the aisle with her head low.

> JEFF
> (TO SOFIA)
> You don't hav-tuh do that you know.

Sofia looks up at Jeff with a mixture of embarrassment and anger.

> SOFIA
> What do you mean?

> JEFF
> I use-tuh tell jokes to make people
> like me, but they didn't respect me

> SOFIA
> Yeah, Thanks for that.

CUT TO:

EXT. BIG BEND NATIONAL PARK - CONTINUOUS

Students walk the trail in groups. Most talk. Some journal.

Sofia falls behind to catch her breath. Her eyes drift over the landscape as her breathing slows.

A reflecting light in the sand draws her attention.

She glances in the direction of her class; the last group walks out of sight.

SOFIA

It's not like they'll notice if I'm
gone.

Amelia and Emil hide behind a boulder watching Sofia leave the trail. Smug smiles overtake their faces.

AMELIA

Oh, let's bust her!

EMIL

Why don't we see what she found
first?

AMELIA

(NODS HER HEAD)

If it's worth anything, we keep it.

CUT TO:

EXT. BIG BEND NATIONAL PARK - CONTINUOUS

A corner of a tin lunch box sticks out of the ground. Recognition dawns on Sofia's face as she unearths it.

SOFIA

(TO HERSELF)

Dad's gonna love this!

A stylized image of Harrison Ford in a fedora with the text INDIANA JONES AND THE TEMPLE OF DOOM lays across the front.

CUT TO:

EXT. BIG BEND NATIONAL PARK - CONTINUOUS

The Ruiz twins walk behind Sofia as she kneels over her find.

AMELIA
Whatcha got there, <u>Sofa</u> Queen?

Sofia gasps and drops the lunchbox. The clamor echoes off the nearby rocks and the impact forces the lid open.

The three students stare in shocked amazement at the contents.

EMIL
Is that what I think it is?

JEFF WALKER (O.S.)
Unfortunately for you, it is.

Jeff Walker appears from behind a boulder. His handgun points at the kids. He appears distressed and shaky. Confusion captures the children's faces.

SOFIA
Mr. Walker? What are you doing?

JEFF
(SHAKING HIS HEAD)
I really wish ya hadn't found that... Hadn't opened it especially. Hand it over, Sofia.

Jeff takes the lunchbox and gestures with his handgun off the trail down a gully, avoiding their eye contact as tears well in his eyes.

JEFF
Alright, off the trail, now.

SOFIA
Where are you taking us?

JEFF
I'm sorry kids. I ain't got much of a choice, ya see. Comeon.

CUT TO:

EXT. BIG BEND NATIONAL PARK - MOMENTS LATER

The students huddle together as Jeff Walker paces back and forth, gun in one hand and cell phone to his ear on the other talking pleadingly with the other. The students whimper and visibly shake with fright.

JEFF
But they's kids sir...

Jeff pauses as the unknown voice speaks unheard threats. Sweat gleans off his face and he continues to wipe tears from his eyes.

JEFF
(cont'd)
Please don't say that. I'll... I'll take care of it

The phone call ends and Jeff Walker looks at the kids in front of him. He points the gun shakily at them.

JEFF
I really wish I didn't have-tuh, honest. But it's my only way out.

Jeff sniffles and turns his head to rub his eyes again. Sofia suddenly shoves Emil into Amelia and dives sideways for a large rock. Jeff reacts by firing a shot that grazes Sofia's arm.

She throws the rock at Jeff, striking him in the head. The twins rush Jeff; Amelia pries the box out of one hand while Emil fights for the gun in the other.

JEFF
(STUNNED) (CONT'D)
Lemme Go! Gitoff!

Emil throws the gun in the opposite direction as the three run for the trail. Sofia's arm pours blood.

                            EMIL
            What did he mean 'his only way out?' You
             think he's in the mob or something?!

                            SOFIA
                I dunno! Let's get outta here!

EXT. BIG BEND NATIONAL PARK - MOMENTS LATER

Jeff pursues the 8th graders, desperation and madness in his
eyes and blood running down his face. His eye swells from the
bloodied gash along his cheek bone. The gun has been replaced
with a hunter's knife. The students close in on the trail as Jeff
closes in on the kids.

                            KIDS
                Help! He's going to kill us!

Jeff grabs Amelia's wrist and yanks the box from her.

He threatens Amelia with the knife as a tour group approaches.
A PARK RANGER (female, 20s) draws her sidearm.

                        PARK RANGER
            Drop the weapon and step away from the kids!

Panic seizes Jeff's body as his hands shoot up and the knife
drops. Tears streamed down his face.

                            SOFIA
                He tried to kill us for this. We
                   found it off the trail.

The Ranger opens the box, her eyes widening in surprise.

                                                    CUT TO:

INT. A HOSPITAL - NIGHT

Sofia looks at the flowers and card in the twins' hands.

AMELIA
(CRYING)
I'm so sorry for everything. I've been terrible, and you saved our lives.

SOFIA
(SHRUGS)
I let it happen, but never again.

AMELIA
(WIPES HER TEARS; NODS)
Thank you, Sofie

EMIL
(TO THE FLOOR)
Yah, thanks.

FADE OUT.

DESTINY HAS IT

Genre: Romance

Word: Lower

Action: Dyeing Hair

Tyrell had no intention of meeting anyone. He had one day in Dallas for business and then Ft. Worth next morning. Yet, here he sat with a woman whose green eyes suggested this bar was exactly where he needed to be.

"I feel like... I've known you my whole life," he stammered. "Is there anything we don't have in common?"

She smiled perfectly, "Oh, you'd be surprised."Tyrell looked at his watch, "Listen, I need to finish some work. Is there a way I could meet you back here around 10:30?"

"I'm across the street in Room 212. You should come by."

His eyebrows raised, "I'm actually one floor up! Seems like destiny's on our side."

She lowered her head shyly, "I'm glad we've met!"

He had everything wrapped up and in his rental by 10:05. It had been a while since his heart pounded after a job, but his mind raced to see her.

Room 212's door was unlatched so Ty pushed it open. "Hey Lessane, I know I'm early but I figured..."

His voice trailed. A man laid bound on Lesanne's bed with a plastic bag duct-taped over his head. She was dyeing her hair black at the sink when she caught his reflection.

"You're early!" Her voice hardened, "I'm sorry you've seen this, I didn't want to kill you..."

His knowing grin confused her, "It seems *we do* have a lot in common," he said, "Suffocation has less blood, but it's easier to move a body in pieces."

ONE MINUTE TILL THE END OF THE WORLD

Start the story with the first line "Lily unlocked the back door of the thrift store using a key that didn't belong to her."

Lily unlocked the back door of the thrift store using a key that didn't belong to her. The key belonged to the old man she'd pickpocketed earlier in the evening. Unbeknownst to Lily, however, neither the owner nor the thrift store belonged to Earth.

She moved through the cluttered wood-paneled 1970s style office quickly. Her score waited for her in the jewelry case by the registers.She passed the nostalgic VHS and DVD section, the used clothes that smelled of her Nana's house, and the stacks of mismatched dishes. Lily set to work on the locked case like a seasoned surgeon opening a patient's chest for the thousandth time. The glass door opened, Lily's fingers plucked the various pieces in darkness along the silk-lined bed with the dexterity of a concert pianist and placed them onto various hooks within her over-the-shoulder bag. It was only when her middle finger caught a slight dimple in the silk that she paused. It cupped the tip of her finger perfectly. *Too perfect.* She pressed the divet and a distinct *click* released the spring latch that held the false bottom secure.

Sliding it out of the way revealed a fist-sized stone inset in velvet. Its dark red hue and tear-shaped design made it look like blood. Her heart quickened as her hands lifted it from its setting. An unexpected warmth rushed through her like the first sip of coffee on a bitter cold February day.

The store's alarm snapped Lily's attention with an ear-splitting shriek. *It can't be.* She had checked the alarm to the thrift store before entering, and it had not been set. Still, instinct moved her hands over her ears and her legs out the front door of the thrift store. Outside the alarm seemed louder; So loud, in fact, that two dancers at the Peacock Cabaret across the street covered their ears. Despite the ten o'clock hour, the sky pulsed an emerald green in time with the alarm.

"It's," Lily realized, "Not coming from the store?" Before she could comprehend further, the siren abruptly cut off. She and the ecdysiasts pulled their hands away looking at each other. An automated message spoke from everywhere at once, "Citizens, immigrants, and travelers of Earth. Please remain calm. The Palez has been removed. Earth is under a Class I restriction for all interplanetary travel and a Class II restriction for all planetary travel. If not restored within one Earth minute, atmospheric discharge will occur. Thank you." The voice cut off as abruptly as it started. The sky, though no longer pulsing, remained brilliantly green. Lily looked from the performers to the stone in her hand. "Surely..." she began, but was cut off as a suctioning sound thrummed into action.

Within fifteen seconds, the air rushed upwards, pulling her and the performers' hair straight up as if they were all in a free fall. Twenty seconds in had Lily gasping for air as if she were on top of Mount Everest. With only a basic cocktail of deduction and survival, she ran with all the speed of a turtle through molasses to the thrift store's door. Thirty five seconds passed and Lily's intestines tried to escape her throat as she fumbled to the pilfered jewelry case. At fifty three seconds, Lily's brain felt like gravy on a biscuit. She pawed for the hidden button, re-releasing the compartment. At sixty seconds her world went black.

"Palez restoral complete. Earth reset complete. Thank you."

Lily gasped back into consciousness on the floor of a thrift store that didn't belong to her. She bolted upright at the revelation of being alive, though the motion made her head want to explode. Pulling herself upwards, the hidden compartment closed over the Palez stone. Wobbling outside, the sky had returned to its inky dark self and the strippers stood talking like any other smoke break. She staggered across the street to them, "Are you okay? What the hell, right?" The two exchanged glances with each other and looked at Lily with eyebrows scrunched, "Hon, what are you talking about?"

IGGRASH THE (ALMOST) INVINCIBLE

Genre: Sci-fi/Fantasy

Object: Deodorant

Setting: Starts on a cliff

ONE - FORTUNATE

The sword's tip dragged through the dirt, its hilt clinging to a gnarly gray-green hand with jagged fingernails. The sword and its goblin owner trudged towards the Cliffs of Visril. His amber eyes focused down his pointed nose towards his boots. The smell of seared flesh from the branded "X" on his cheek made his stomach curl.

"'Iggrash the Fearful.' Hrmph!" his graveled voice betrayed his hurt as he swore, "Elf-shik."

Slouching at the edge of the cliff, he scowled at the waves crashing against the rocks below, "Can't believin' they banishin' me fir wantin' not to be torn apart by lycan-folk." The tumult below beckoned to him, "Supposin' I'd go someways soon anyways. At least when rocks bitin' I can't be turnin' intuh one."

His foot swung out over nothing and his eyes closed. He leaned forward to accept his fate.

"Urf!" The sudden impact to his head turned him around, anticipating a foe. His sword stood guard, "Showin' your face, coward!" Only the warblers and horned frogs filled his elongated ears. His sword hand lowered as his other rose to rub the new bump on his head, "What hittin' me?"

It didn't take long to find the source. Iggrash's bristled eyebrows raised and his near toothless mouth gaped. There against the grass, what looked like an elongated robin's egg drew his eye, "What's it?" *Clack.* His blade poked the hard thing, and Iggrash's eyebrows dropped to a furrowed stance. He crouched down and extended an elongated fingernail towards it, *Clack.*

Picking it up, his eyebrows maintained their inquisitive stance. "Not bein' stone or iron," he pondered, "Glass?" He frowned at this, shaking his head, "Almost. Almost glass." His finger traced the ovoid shape of the almost-glass. Near the rounded end, it had a ridge while the flatter end had some sort of knob.

Turning the thing over, various inscriptions were imprinted on it. "Hsss!" He dropped it quickly as if it had burned him, "Man-speak!" Though he recognized the words immediately, he could only understand some of them: *24 hr protection. Solid. Secret. Lavender. Aluminum Zirconium Trichlorohydrex. Deodorant. Net Wt. 1.7 oz (48 g).*

"Must bein' some incantation of wizard or witch." He looked around again, expecting said conjurer to appear from behind a tree to turn him to stone, but none did. Looking upwards only revealed the purple clouds of an oncoming storm. He studied the first line above the ridge: *24 hr protection.* Though never accused of intelligence, Iggrash wasn't so dimwitted that he couldn't understand that word. *Protection.*

Like it did with every goblin, greed compelled him. He picked up the almost-glass with curious anticipation. Looking closer, he was surprised he could see through the top curved part and that a white base lay inside it. When he turned the knob at the bottom, the white base rose. "There bein' the magic." His eyes flicked to the largest word. *Secret.* "Must bein' a trick to get it." He looked further down and cackled, "Ay! The spell!" He spoke the words eagerly, "Alum-in-um. Zircon-i-um. Tri..." He stared at the last word in disbelief. This word seemed far from the man-speak he knew.

"Elf-shik!" he cursed the bottle, "Give me your elixir, Secret deo-dorant!" He tore at it with a frenzy until his fingernails caught the ridge and the upper part popped off.

The earthy floral scent bombarded his oversized nostrils and replaced his frustration with calm. "It drawin' me down," he stared at the white powdery substance in awe. An attempted smile stretched across his face. Without waiting for instruction, his forked tongue slithered from between his teeth and dragged over the powder. Instantly retreating into his mouth, his tongue pulled on the back of the throat forcing him to retch.

After regaining himself, Iggrash continued his examination. The scent again tempted him, though his tongue remembered well enough and stayed where it belonged. This time, he slid his finger across the top. It felt soft and slick and when he turned it over, his finger had the faintest shimmer to it. "It hurtin' not." The scent perfumed off his finger. His eyebrows raised as his simple mind thought through it. *Protection.* A simple epiphany lighted the dim bulb of his mind, "It bein' armor?" His eyes flicked to the largest word. *Secret.* He nodded his head, the ghastly grin cracking his face again, "None can be seein' it."

Within moments, the lavender aroma radiated from every part of the odious goblin's skin. Feeling empowered, he lifted his sword to the heavens and proclaimed, "Iggrash the Invincible!" As if to test his claim, the heavens responded by delivering him a bolt of lightning.

Iggrash the Lucky woke to a relentless beating of rain on his face and the faint smell of something burning. "Urgh," was the only thing he could manage as he sat up. The smoke billowed off his hooded tunic. He pat himself and wiggled his limbs in a quick medical assessment, "I'm livin'?" His gappy-toothed grin returned, "I'm livin'!" The thunder roared an ominous warning, shooting Iggrash to his feet, "Timin' to move."

TWO - FOOLISH

The weather persisted, but Iggrash's mind lingered on his escape from death. Trudging through the wilderness, he came upon a clearing where an angelic voice chimed through the downpour, "Long way from home, aren't you?" A second voice answered, "But Nym, don't you see, this one doesn't have a home!" The first voice mocked, "Poor thing's been banished by his own kind, Farryn!" Iggrash's hand rose subconsciously towards the "X" on his cheek as the laughter sang out. Those voices did not belong to any angels. *Elf-beings.*

He crept forward, lurking behind trees. On the opposite edge of the clearing, two elvish soldiers in blinding white armor had a young goblin cornered between the two of them shoving him back and forth.

Iggrash's old instinct encouraged him to flee from the scene when the lavender on his body caught his nose. *Secret. Protection. Secret Protection.* Now the scent seemed to empower him and Iggrash the Foolish drew his sword and charged into the open clearing.

More amused than surprised, Nym and Farryn watched the lone goblin burst from the thicket of the woods with its sword leading the charge. "What do you suppose his plan is, Nym?"

Smiling, Nym removed his bow from his shoulder, "I think he means to kill us, Farryn."

"Master of surprise isn't he?" Farryn's smile glistened.

Nym reached leisurely towards his quiver, "A true tactician, brother." 75 yards separated the charging goblin from the elves.

Farryn eyed the creature with apathy, "Where do you aim?"

"I'll stick him through the left eye."

The goblin closed the distance to 65 yards and Nym nocked his arrow and took his time sighting his mark; 50 yards.

The arrow launched like a predator pouncing on its prey. Nym's arrogant disinterest changed to genuine surprise when the advancing creature tripped and fell face first in the split moment before the arrow hit its target; 46 yards. The maddened being scrambled up and pawed at his eyes, moving an erratic five yards closer. Farryn bemused, "He can't see for the mud smeared across his eyes."

In a flash, Nym drew and loosed another arrow only to have it miss its mark. The bumbling goblin staggered two steps to the right as the missile flew past. Drawing his third and final arrow, he steadied himself, "His fortune ends here." 30 yards.

"RARGH!" The shout from his left preceded a searing light to Nym's eyes followed by darkness.

Farryn turned in time to see the goblin-child smashing a rock into his brother's head, sending the loaded arrow wide. "Nym!" Knocking the changeling to the ground Farryn drew his sword, the rage and disbelief rising, "You'll regret that, you filth!"

Before he could deliver on his promise, Farryn's eyes and mouth opened in surprise as the blade slid between two plates in his armor and punctured his lung. He gasped only one word, "How?" as he looked around at the muddied goblin. "*Secret,*" the vile thing grinned."

Iggrash looked from the fallen elves to the goblin-child's face. The "X" was an older wound than his own, shinier and white. "Namin'?" Iggrash growled.

"Ort. You?"

"Iggrash the Invincible."

The two sized each other up in silent disdain, until Ort spoke again, "Why you smellin' of Nymph?"

Iggrash's hand clutched briefly at the pouch around his belt before moving it away. The changeling's greedy eyes caught the motion, "What havin' you there?"

"Nothin' bein', you!" Iggrash reached out and smacked at the hungry eyes, knocking the young one down, "I takin' leave and needin' no company."

Iggrash started away when Ort spoke again, suspiciously, "Ne'er met a goblin that didn't takin' what's won before." Iggrash looked back to Ort already dismantling Nym's shining-white armor. His own greed crept back up, "I enjoyin' the take." Iggrash hoped he didn't sound too defensive.

He snatched a dagger from Farryn's belt and tucked it into his own boot and stood to leave again.

"Just the poke?" Ort's question seemed accusing.

The flesh wound on his cheek burned fresh as Iggrash continued walking, "Too much take bringin' too much attention." Without another word, Iggrash left the goblin-child to his plunder.

THREE - INSANE

The barrage of rain made navigating impossible, but even without it, Iggrash would have had no idea where he was headed. His entire day's (and life's) plan had changed when the mysterious almost-glass hit him in the head. So when he saw the dim lights, he figured it was as good a direction as any. He pushed out of the thicket and almost ran into the oak sign-post marked **ORC-HOL**. "Orcs. *Ptoo*." The thick spit dribbled slowly down the sign as he proceeded into the town.

Orcs and goblins weren't exactly enemies, but they weren't exactly allies either. There had been orcs that fought alongside goblins in the Lycan War, but it was usually so they could throw a goblin in between themselves and the were-creatures.

Through the rain, the adobe buildings with their lamp flickering windows looked like ancient golems trying to push through the earth. Iggrash trudged between them, his boots sucking mud with every step.

He looked with little interest at each window, until his ears picked up the distinct sound of a harpsichord echoing across the rain. He followed it to a hanging sign marked *Gra's Grog*. Peering into the window, Iggrash counted 7 orcs from left to right; one tending bar, one drinking in front of it, four at a table in the middle playing dice, and a harpsichordist on the far wall.

The Lavender scent caught Iggrash's nose and allowed a mischievous grin to spread across his face.

"Better doublin' deo-dorant, I'm thinkin'." Hunched under the awning, Iggrash reapplied the protecting powder as a glint shimmered in his eye. Satisfied with the lavender aurora, he slunk inside.

He never detected the other figure lingering in the shadows watching him with a growing curiosity.

Gra specifically built his bar with only one way in and out. This allowed his one good eye to spot trouble from the door while he faced his patrons; Had he seen a goblin enter, he would've shot the vermin dead with the crossbow he kept under the counter. It happened that Gra turned his good eye away at the precise moment when Iggrash the Insane entered.

Iggrash crept towards the drunk at the bar as the lavender smell listed idly over to the dice players. Given that lavender did not exist in their land, no one could have known just how highly allergic orcs were to the flora's aroma. Ensnaring the nearest orc by the nostrils, the odor forced a hard sneeze.

Later goblin-lore would speculate on the actual events that unfolded that night. The following is the most accepted version of Iggrash and the Seven Orcs.

Sneezy's snot flew at the hairy orc next to him. Hairy retaliated by shoving him backward.

Seconds prior, Iggrash ripped the barstool from under the drunk orc's posterior at the bar. Being inebriated and taken by surprise, Drinky's chin received a K.O. uppercut from the bartop. The barstool's backward momentum met the recently toppled Sneezy's head, leaving both the barstool and Sneezy down for the count.

It is important to note that at this point all orcs still conscious became aware that there was, in fact, a goblin in the room.

Said goblin trampolined off Drinky's unconscious body toward the orc sitting across the table from Hairy. The orc being lunged at was too slow to react as he was still processing why there was a goblin in the bar.

Iggrash landed on his target's head and exchanged multiple right and left hooks across Slowy's face. Being in direct contact with the lavender-laced goblin, Slowy's throat closed as he pawed at his assailant.

For the first time, an orc found an opportunity to take the offensive. The bald one next to the skirmish yanked Iggrash off Slowy's bludgeoned face. Covering his face with his free hand, Baldy stood and held the goblin at arm's distance.

Meanwhile, Slowy's violent coughing reeled him backward, planting his head firmly into the adobe wall.

From the bar, Gra fired his crossbow at Iggrash. Missing its mark by two inches, the bolt instead punctured Baldy's massive outstretched arm, allowing the goblin to drop to the table.

The Harpsichordist and Hairy dove for the insolent insurgent, their heads colliding with each other with a dull *smack*, rendering each other incapacitated.

Standing on top of the table, his grin spread ear to ear and his hands raised in victory, "IGGRASH THE INVINC--" a second crossbow bolt interrupted his battle cry as it swooshed past his face. Cackling, the goblin jumped to the door towards his escape.

Up until this day, glee had been as foreign as the deodorant in his pouch. Darting through the alleys, "Iggrash the Invincible" prattled repeatedly from his lips, the idiotic grin becoming a more permanent fixture on his face.

Between the rain and his mantra, Iggrash didn't see the plank of wood till it was an inch from his face.

FOUR - DEFEATED

For the second time that day, Iggrash found himself coming-to in the rain. This time, the taste of blood filled his mouth. "I sein' ya goin' in and out the orc drinkin' hole."

Still reeling, Iggrash opened his eyes to see his own blade pointed at his throat. His eyes traced the iron up towards the hilt and the small goblin hand holding it. Through the rain, he could make out the young face with the familiar branded scar.

"Ort?"

Ort snarled, "Been wonderin' why you didn't care for the takin'. Only figurin' is must bein' havin' some kinda *secret*." The last word came out like a slap. "This bein' protection incantation? I seein' how you smearin' it o'er you." Ort appraised the deodorant that he held out in his other hand.

Outrage spewed from Iggrash, "It bein' mine, thief!" Ort cocked his head in mocked surprise, "But for the rules of the takin', it seemin' like it bein' mine?"

Ptoo! Igrrash spit blood across Ort's face. Ort pressed the sword against Iggrash's neck, "You bein' lucky you savin' me prior. For that, I returnin' the deed." Ort backed away slowly keeping the sword at arms length between the two of them, "I keepin' these though."

At that, Ort turned and disappeared into the rain forever. All Iggrash knew was that he wanted to pursue and wring the little changeling's neck, but his brain swam and his limbs felt like pudding. The rain swallowed his voice, "Goblin trash!"

The rain drummed on his pounding skull as trudged aimlessly. When the clouds parted, the day-star was already kissing the horizon and the smell of lavender had all but dissipated, with only faint whiffs coming through.

Whether by design or destiny, Iggrash found himself back at the Cliffs of Visril, in nearly the same spot. "Rotten goblin-filth," he spewed, "Takin' what's given me."

Looking skyward, Iggrash's fists clenched as he shouted, "Why choosin' Iggrash the Fearful? Already bein' a wretch and coward not enough?!" His feet paced back and forth, "Choosin' to laugh at Iggrash rather?"

Hot tears streamed down his face, "WHY BEIN' ME?!" he pleaded, "ANSWERIN' ME!!!" The indifferent heavens cared not for the wrath of the dust speck. The tears flowed now; had he not already been banished for his cowardice, he most certainly would have been killed for this un-goblin show of emotion.

Dusk retreated into darkness and the sister full moons took the place of the day-star.

With no other recourse, humiliation and shame encouraged him towards the cliff's edge for the last time. He'd taken only a couple of steps, when the heavy rustle of brush behind stopped him hard.

The growl vibrated through the earth and up his spine. The warm, moist breath on the back of his neck sent icy shivers down his body. Against all his instincts, he turned to see the wolf-man standing on its hind legs, baring its teeth. The lycan knocked Iggrash flying into a tree. The behemoth barreled down on him, a demonic hunger lusting in its eyes.

Though he'd have believed it impossible to be distracted by anything with a werewolf charging him, a brilliant glint from his boot caught the moonlights. Recognition hit him and his fingers fumbled for the white metal as his eyes fixated in horror at the hulking beast barreling upon him, claws and teeth yearning for blood.

The silver flash preceded the agonizing howl by a tenth of a second. The beast writhed and pawed at the elven dagger embedded in its nose. Iggrash pressed backward against the tree, watching with macabre fascination.

The lycanthrope found purchase on the dagger and pulled. Its head yanked back, sending its momentum over the cliff face to its death below.

Stunned, Iggrash slunk to the edge. The behemoth's silhouette spasmed against the dark outlines of jutted rocks. For a brief moment, he could only stare.

"Supposin' I'd go someways, someday," he considered, " not bein' today and not bein' that ways."

With that, Iggrash the Endurer turned away from the Cliffs of Visril, vowing to never return.

FIVE - EPILOGUED

"Hey mom, can you buy me some deodorant at the store?"

"Really, Tasha? Again?"

"I'm not doing it on purpose!"

"I swear if I find you're hoarding them somewhere..."

"Why would I do that?!"

"I have no idea what kids do these days. I read about that Tide Pod challenge a few years ago..."

"That was one kid, and Ew! I'm not eating deodorant! Why would you think that?"

"Well what else are you doing with them?"

"YOU MEAN BESIDES CLEANING MY ARMPITS?"

Sigh. "Really, Tasha. How do they get lost?"

"I don't know! I take it to school, put it in my locker to use for gym, and then it's gone! It's probably that ugly B* that has a locker next to me..."

"Mouth young lady!"

"I'm just saying, Yesterday my favorite lip gloss all of a sudden disappeared after I left it in my locker. Plus there's all the other stuff disappearing."

"Oh don't be so dramatic. You probably let someone borrow them and forgot who you lent them to."

"Ugh, Momm-uh. I'm telling the truth..."

Pop.

"Where'd you find it?"

Pop.

"In the alley behind Gra's when I went lookin' for that goblin-shik."

Pop.

"Well don't hog it!"

Hairy had barely applied the Honest Beauty Gloss-C Lip Gloss's wand to his snarled lips, before Sneezy yanked it away. The disheveled orcs snatched it back and forth from each other, enjoying the satisfying smacking noise the sticky shimmery goo made on their lips.

Pop.

ACKNOWLEDGEMENT

I recognize this is only a self-published book that may never see very many eyes, but there are certain eyes I want to make sure to see and know how much I appreciate them.

First of course goes to my wife, Aleena. Without her, I would have given up long ago on this writing journey. I am blessed to have been provided by God and the Universe with a partner that understands my vision, that allows me to vent my frustrations and fears, but also refuses to let me get completely self-depreciative. As cliche as it is, she's been my rock and solid ground. She has been there with me the entire time, reading every story or paragraph or sentence that I've given her. She's been able to provide umpteenth amounts of helpful criticism that has made my stories better.

To my family. My parents, Gabe and Debbie Figueroa have always encouraged me to question the world around me and have been incredibly supportive early readers of my work. To my siblings, Micah and Ruben Figueroa, and Hannah Callis - I love you all and thank you for again being supporters and readers of my work (even though I know you kinda have to).

To my first, and so far only, writers' group: *Haribol Writers!* Thank you Krishna Priya, Naveen Jani, Devika Rao, and Gopi Gita-Shomaker for the support and constructive criticism of my first completed story. Without this community of support, it would have taken a lot longer to decide to put my work out there. Perhaps one day we can reunite, all of us successful and accomplished writers.

Next, to my earliest readers and, dare I say it, fans. After my wife, I trusted my stories with select people before I submitted them in contests or to publications. Whitney Loignon, Ashleigh Hill, Jordana Cole, Nathalie Aidarous, Radhika Ramana, Alex Valdez, Adair Spotswood, Matthew and Paige Stephens; thank you. Your excitement over reading my stories has encouraged me to keep going. It is because of you that I know that I am at least a halfway decent storyteller.

And finally, to my kids. You two are always watching me, waiting to see what I'll do. You may not know it yet, but you both are my most compelling reason to keep writing. I hope that I can show you how to work towards a worthwhile dream so that you both can believe in your own dreams to pursue.

ABOUT THE AUTHOR

Ryan G. Figueroa

Ryan is an award-winning author, world renowned story-teller, celebrated public speaker, and inspiration to the masses. He also believes that one day these things will become true. At the moment of this publishing, he is, at the very least, relentlessly optimistic.

He does believe in the power of vision casting as well as understanding the "why" behind doing anything. For him, his "why" is simple: To work in the uncomfortable towards his own goals, so that others will see his light and feel compelled to shine too.

Currently, he is a writer with a full time job carrying mail and lives with his wife and two kids near Dallas, Tx. When he can, he enjoys going to movies, reading both fiction and non-fiction, and keeping in shape.

www.ingramcontent.com/pod-product-compliance
Lightning Source LLC
Chambersburg PA
CBHW071235170626
46809CB00008BA/3076